Living Love Forward

I Don't Understand What You Are Saying

I0559556

Book of Idioms

A Children's Leadership Series

Written by Kim Dawson

Illustrated by Paige Anocibar

Publisher: Tandem Services Press
PO Box 220, Yucaipa, CA 92399
www.tandemservicesink.com

Book Design by Paige Anocibar

ISBN 978-1-954986-26-8

Appreciation to

Inland Leaders Charter School and all our teachers and staff for inspiring and supporting me to write this series.

All my students and their families who taught me to be a better teacher and person.

Eduardo, a former student, for letting me borrow his awesome name.

The 2nd, 3rd, 4th, and 5th grade classes at Inland Leaders that gave me GREAT feedback, which strengthened my story.

Pelican Elementary in Oregon for letting us use their school as a model for Lexie's Huckleberry Elementary.

Leanne Cullen at Pelican Elementary for inspiring me to create a new character (Mrs. Carlton, the lunch lady).

Ruth Chamberlin for letting me borrow her artwork for the hallways of Huckleberry Elementary (Pelican mural).

My family and friends who have never wavered in supporting and encouraging my mission to help others.

Paige, my illustrator, for putting up with my "creative" tangents.

Jennifer Crosswhite, my editor and friend, who has been my sounding board and always keeps me positive when I hit the many bumps in the road. (https://www.tandemservicesink.com)

All my readers who have supported me and helped me spread the message that kids can be leaders too.

Sending a ton of love and encouragement to all of you!
We got this!

From the author of the series Living Love Forward:

I wrote this children's leadership series to create an open conversation about the experiences our kids face every day. Being a teacher for over two decades, I have created connections with kids of all ages. I have observed and learned a lot through these interactions and have discovered key skill sets that I think are important for their growth. My purpose in writing these sentimental and caring stories is the hope that they instill life skills and resilience in our children. In turn, this empowers them to become successful and compassionate people, as well as strong leaders. Join Lexie and our children as they navigate this journey of self-discovery.

Please note that this series can be used in conjunction with any Leadership Program focused on survival skills and effective habits for children.

This book specifically focuses on:

- **Idioms**
- **English language learners**
- **Anxiety**
- **Frustration**
- **Negative attitude**
- **Self-esteem**
- **Resilience**
- **Patience**
- **Compassion**

Map of Harlow

Train Station

Church Of Hope

Liberty Library

Cemetery

1st Street
2nd Street
2nd Street
3r
Rose Road
Daisy Lane
4th Street
Main Street

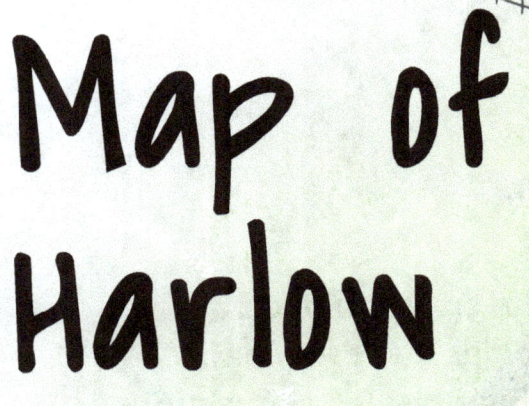

Lexie's House

Bus Stop

4th St

Rose Road

Main Street

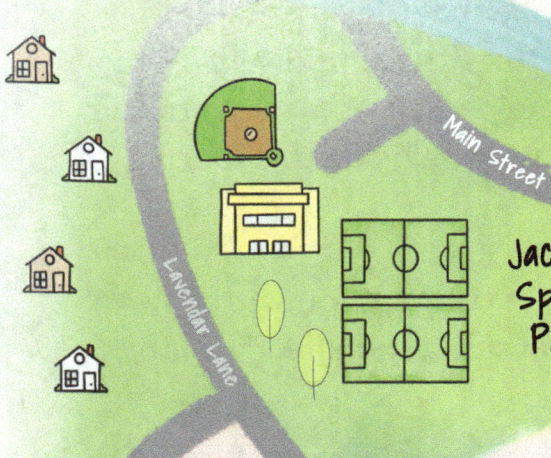

Main Street

Jackson Sports Park

Lavendar Lane

Jasmine Avenue

Riverside Park

Lotus Loop

Lavender Lane

Rose Road

Huckleberry Elementary

Lotus Loop

Lavendar Lane

Jasmine Avenue

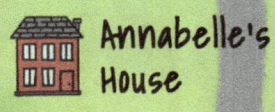

Annabelle's House

Jasmine Avenue

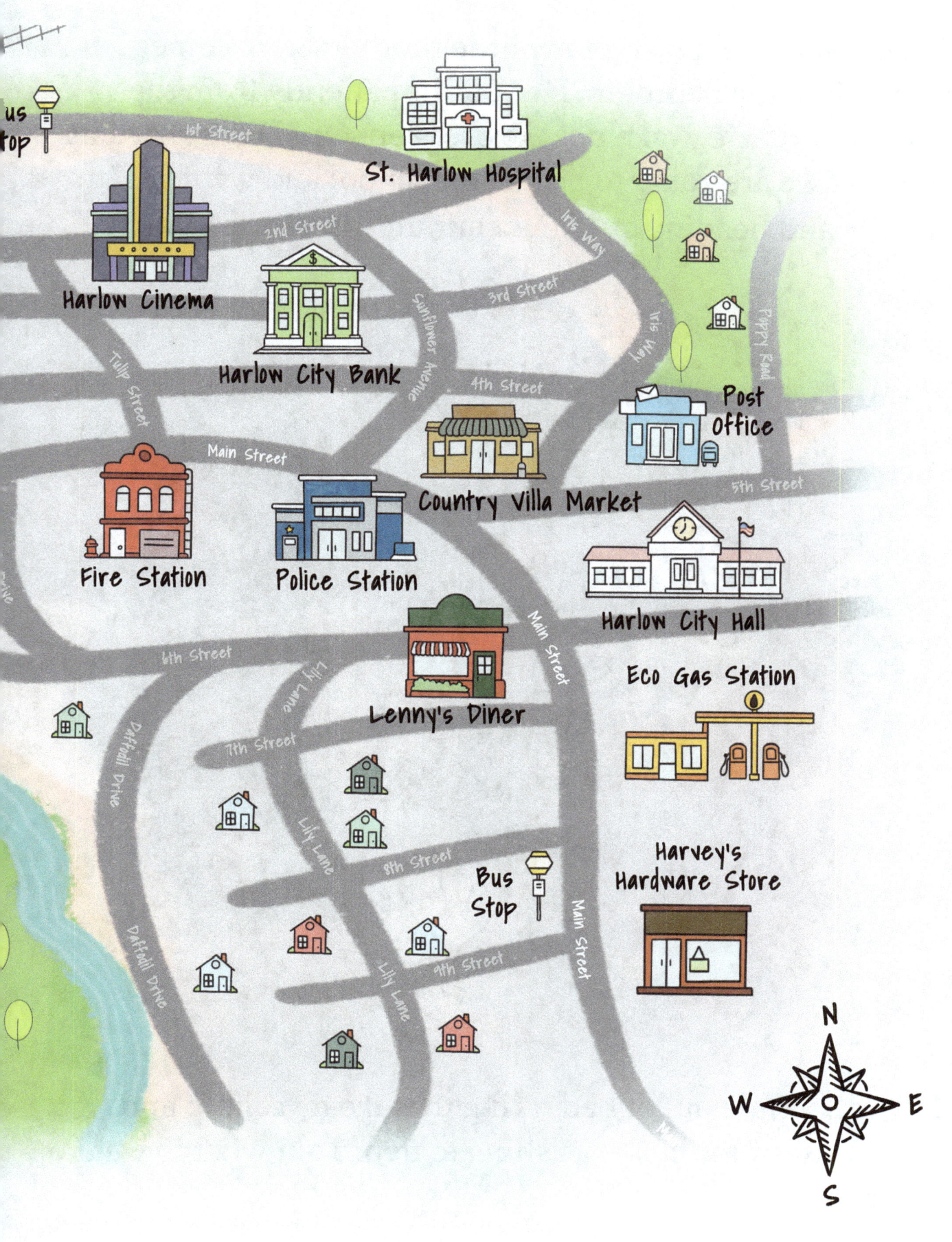

I awaken abruptly when my little brother, Sam, comes racing into my bedroom. He yells impatiently from the doorway, "Lexie, wake up! We overslept and Dad's stressing out that we are going to be late for school and wants us in the car and heading out in ten minutes! You better hurry!"

I **groggily** slide out of bed trying to wake myself up and then ransack my closet, rushing to figure out what to wear for the day.

I dress quickly as I rush downstairs into the kitchen, and Dad hands me a piece of toast as he grabs his car keys. "What happened, Dad?" I ask as I follow him out the front door.

"The alarm didn't go off and now we are late. Hurry up, you guys!" he shouts as we all hurry to the car.

We make it to school just as the bell is ringing and race to class. I slip into my seat and take a breath while glancing around the room. I notice a new student is sitting at a desk near the windows and he is looking kind of scared and intimidated. Mrs. Bryce, my teacher, walks to the front of the room and says, "Good morning, class. Buenos Dias."

We all say, "Good morning, Mrs. Bryce." while looking at
her a little confused, because she has never greeted us that
way before. I notice the new kid doesn't say anything, but
he does look up and smile at Mrs. Bryce. She looks at him
thoughtfully and then introduces him to the class.

"Class, this is Eduardo and he just moved here from Mexico. He doesn't know a lot of English and he will be learning it with us in class." She commends him by saying, "What is amazing about Eduardo is that once he learns English, he will be a dual speaker, which means he will be able to speak both English AND Spanish. What a remarkable feat." Then she turns to him and welcomes him by saying, "Bienvenido a clase, Eduardo."

"Gracias,...thank you, gracias," Eduardo says shyly while glancing up at her.

She then turns to me and says, "Lexie, I want you to be Eduardo's buddy and show him around. Maybe you can introduce him to some of the kids and help him with any questions he might have."

"Okay, Mrs. Bryce," I say. I turn to him and smile and he gives me a shy smile in return.

Mrs. Bryce has Eduardo move desks so he is sitting next to me. She works with him for a bit, introducing him to a computer program that works on building his English vocabulary and then she starts our morning warm-up activity. Throughout the morning, I watch and listen as Mrs. Bryce comes over to work with Eduardo. He knows more English than I suspected. I notice though that he scrunches his nose up and makes a funny face when he is unsure and doesn't understand something. He is resilient though and keeps trying. Soon it is time for lunch.

As we make our way to the lunch area, I say to Eduardo, "I am starving. Let's go pig out!" Eduardo's nose scrunches up, but I didn't notice.

As we head down the hallway, we look through the windows and see it is raining really hard outside. One of the kids passes by us and calls out to another kid, "Man, do you see that? It is raining cats and dogs out there!" Eduardo looks back and forth from the window to the kid and scrunches his face up again, I didn't notice. We keep walking and I show him where we line up for lunch.

As we are waiting our turn, Jason, the school bully, comes over and I hold my breath. I stood up to him a while back and he has left me alone, but Eduardo is new. As he approaches us, he calls out, "I heard there was a new kid at school. What's your name?"

Eduardo looks at him in confusion and I know he isn't sure how to answer Jason.

"What's going on...Cat got your tongue?" taunts Jason.

Cat got your tongue?

Eduardo continues to look at Jason with confusion on his face.

"Jason," I say, "this is Eduardo and he is new and doesn't speak a lot of English. He doesn't understand what you are saying and you are picking on him. We have already had this conversation about how you need to stop being mean to people. Remember, you told me your dad wouldn't want you to do that."

Jason looks at me for a long moment remembering this conversation we had a while back.

He holds his hand up as if surrendering and says, "All right... all right!" See!...I am as cool as a cucumber! I definitely don't want to be in hot water with you, Lexie! You are one tough cookie!

See you around, Eduardo. Bye, Lexie." He backs away and goes to join his friends at their table.

We finally get to the front of the line and Eduardo looks around as if not knowing what to do. His eyes land on Mrs. Carlton, our awesome lunch lady, and he moves towards her as she motions him over. She surprises all of us as she starts to hesitantly speak Spanish to him. She is a little unsure but seems determined to talk with him.

"Hola, mi llamo Señora Carlton," Mrs. Carlton says to him. "¿Te gustaría algo de comer? Tenemos macarrones con queso, ensalada, o puedes comer un sándwich aquí." I have no idea what Mrs. Carlton is saying to Eduardo, but she is pointing at the macaroni and cheese, the salad bowls, and the bagged lunches that have sandwiches in them. My guess is she is asking him what he wants to eat.

Eduardo response with a warm smile, "Gracias, mi nombre es Eduardo." I look at him with puzzlement, although I think he is introducing himself to her. "Puedes comer un sándwich, profaner," he says to Mrs. Carlton and she passes him a bagged lunch.

She smiles and says, "Que tengas un buen día, Eduardo. Estoy aquí si necesitas algo."

Mrs. Carlton looks at my confused face and says that she took Spanish in school and remembered a few things. She had heard that morning that we had a new student who spoke Spanish and was watching for him in the lunch line. She continues by sharing that she just told him that if he needs anything to come find her and she will help him.

Gracias.
thank you,
Señora Mrs. Carlton.

He smiles at me and then says to Mrs. Carlton, "Gracias...thank you, Señora...Mrs. Carlton."

I then guide him to the table area and we sit and eat quietly for a while. He eventually turns to me and says, "English is confusing. I don't understand everything that I am hearing."

"Like what?" I ask.

"Why are there cats and dogs falling from the sky?" he asks first in confusion.

I am trying to remember when he heard this and then recall being in the hallway and a kid talking about the rain. "Oh... raining cats and dogs means it is raining REALLY hard," I explain.

He is still looking confused and asks another question, "Why did the boy say a cats got my tongue?" He sticks out his tongue and points to it as he looks at her.

I laugh and say, "Cat got your tongue means 'why aren't you talking?'"...Jason asked you a question and you just looked at him and didn't answer. That's why he said it." He nods slightly. "Are you still confused?" I say with a smile.

He smiles a bit and nods, "Yes, but I think I am understanding. What is it when that boy said you are one tough cookie?" He tilts his head waiting for my answer.

"That means that Jason thinks I am a confident and brave person...that I will stand up for myself," I respond. He nods again.

The rain stops before lunch is over and the yard duties allow us to go outside to play. We finish our lunch quickly, throw away our trash, and head out to recess. As we are walking across the playground, I notice Eduardo scrunching up his face again. I start to listen carefully to what the kids around us are saying. I turn to him and say, "Hey, you have that scrunched up and confused look on your face again that tells me you are confused about something. What don't you understand?"

He points to the basketball court and we hear a kid shouting, "Come on! It's a piece of cake! You can shoot the ball right into the hoop."

I lean towards him as we walk by and say, "It's a piece of cake means it is easy to do. He is telling that boy that he can shoot the ball into the basket."

We continue walking and pass another group of kids talking. One says, "If I do badly on this test,...I am in the same boat. My mom is going to be really mad at me too." Eduardo listens while getting that scrunched up look again.

I am getting good at noticing the look on his face. I lean towards him with questioning eyes and he says, "...in the same boat? There are no boats here?"

I chuckle and say, "It means both of them are in the same situation. Both their moms will be mad at them if they don't get a good grade on their tests. It has nothing to do with a boat."

Eduardo shakes his head in bewilderment and says,

"Then why talk about the boat? This is going to be hard, this English."

The bell eventually rings and we get back to class. Mrs. Bryce asks me how it went at break. I tell her all about how Eduardo kept getting confused by what people were saying. She laughs when I describe the "It's raining cats and dogs" conversation. She leans back in her chair and thinks. She eventually says, "What you are talking about are called idioms." She continues by saying, "An idiom is a phrase that means something different than the actual words being used. They are tricky to understand and comprehend even for people who speak English. I can understand why he is so confused."

idiom (noun)

Mrs. Bryce calls everyone to attention and we continue our day. Eduardo seems to be more comfortable and confident as the day goes on. He even tries to answer one of Mrs Bryce's questions during math time.

He concentrates and speaks slowly, but when no one laughs at him, he seems to feel more comfortable and keeps going.

Riiiiiing!

The bell rings telling us the day is over. I stretch in my seat and hear Mrs. Bryce say, "Let's call it a day, kids! Clean up, stack chairs, and let's skedaddle.

I look towards Eduardo and notice he is smiling and nodding his head.

He doesn't have a scrunched-up face as he turns to me and says, "Let's call it a day means it is time to go home...right?"

"Yes, now you are getting it," I respond. We get up and say goodbye as we leave the classroom.

As I walk towards Dad's car, I think about my day. It has never occurred to me before how many idioms we use in a day when we talk to each other. I started thinking of all the different idioms Mrs. Bryce and I talked about today.

"Wow," I think, "...English really IS hard to understand."

Author's Advice

- Idioms can be fun and funny!

- Show compassion, respect, and patience when helping others.

- We are all beautifully different. It should be celebrated not criticized.

- A little kindness goes a long way.

- Be a good friend.

- Be observant.

Think and Feel

There are several idioms used in this story. Use clues from the story and the page numbers provided to see if you can figure out what the idiom means.

1) **Cat got your tongue** (pg 17): _____

2) **Raining cats and dogs** (pg 16): _____

3) **A piece of cake** (pg 19): _____

4) **A tough cookie** (pg 18): _____

5) **Let's call it a day** (pg 24): _____

MULTIPLE CHOICE
Directions: Look at each idiom, go back into the story, and look for clues about what it means.

6) Idiom: pig out (pg 8)	7) Idiom: cool as a cucumber (pg 12)
A to be in trouble	A to be very calm under stress
B why aren't you talking	B to be in trouble
C easy to do	C time to stop for the day
D to eat a lot	D understanding how someone feels

Glossary

a piece of cake

Definition: it is easy to do

Language Usage:

"a piece of cake" is an idiom
(An idiom is a phrase that means something different than the literal words being used. Examples: "It is raining cats and dogs" means it is raining very hard and "Go break a leg!" means go try your hardest.)

Evidence of how the word is used in the story.

The boys playing basketball at recess yell at a player shooting, "Come on! It's a piece of cake! (It's an easy shot to make.)

be in hot water

Definition: be in trouble; make someone mad at them

Language Usage:

"be in hot water" is an idiom
(An idiom is a phrase that means something different than the literal words being used. Examples: "It is raining cats and dogs" means it is raining very hard and "Go break a leg!" means go try your hardest.)

Evidence of how the word is used in the story.

When Lexie tells Jason, the bully, to stop being mean he says, "I don't want to be in hot water with you!" (I don't want you to be mad at me, Lexie.)

Glossary

bewilderment

Definition: to confuse or puzzle.

Part of Speech:

This word is a (noun, adjective, verb, adverb).

Evidence of how the word is used in the story.

When Lexie tries to explain something to Eduardo, he shakes his head in bewilderment (in confusion).

cat got your tongue

Definition: why aren't you talking

Language Usage:

"cat got your tongue" is an idiom
(An idiom is a phrase that means something different than the literal words being used. Examples: "It is raining cats and dogs" means it is raining very hard and "Go break a leg!" means go try your hardest.)

Evidence of how the word is used in the story.

When Jason, the bully, talks to Eduardo, Eduardo doesn't answer his question. Jason says, "What, a cat got your tongue?" (why aren't you saying anything?)

Glossary

commend

Definition: to speak of with praise for some act or service.

Part of Speech:

This word is a (noun, adjective, verb, adverb).

Evidence of how the word is used in the story.

Mrs. Bryce commends (praises, speaks highly of) Eduardo for becoming a dual speaker in both English and Spanish.

cool as a cucumber

Definition: to be very calm under stress or when challenged

Language Usage:

"cool as a cucumber" is an idiom
(An idiom is a phrase that means something different than the literal words being used. Examples: "It is raining cats and dogs" means it is raining very hard and "Go break a leg!" means go try your hardest.)

Evidence of how the word is used in the story.

When Lexie tells Jason, the bully, to stop being mean he says, "I am as cool as a cucumber" (not a threat and am very calm).

Glossary

feat

Definition: an accomplishment or achievement that shows courage, strength, or skill.

Part of Speech:

This word is a (noun, adjective, verb, adverb).

Evidence of how the word is used in the story.

Mrs Bryce commends Eduardo for learning both English and Spanish. "It will be such an amazing feat" (accomplishment).

groggily

Definition: can not think clearly; unable to wake up

Part of Speech:

This word is a (noun, adjective, verb, adverb).

Evidence of how the word is used in the story.

Lexie struggles to get up in the morning. She groggily (can not think clearly, struggles waking up) slides out of bed, and tries to focus on what she should wear to school.

Glossary

in the same boat

Definition: in the same situation; can understand what other person is going through

Language Usage:

"in the same boat" is an idiom
(An idiom is a phrase that means something different than the literal words being used. Examples: "It is raining cats and dogs" means it is raining very hard and "Go break a leg!" means go try your hardest.)

Evidence of how the word is used in the story.

A group of kids are talking at recess about how they don't want to get in trouble if they don't do well on a test. (they understand the stress of wanting to do well on a test.)

let's call it a day

Definition: time to stop for the day

Language Usage:

"Let's call it a day" is an idiom
(An idiom is a phrase that means something different than the literal words being used. Examples: "It is raining cats and dogs" means it is raining very hard and "Go break a leg!" means go try your hardest.)

Evidence of how the word is used in the story.

When the bell rings at the end of the day, Mrs Bryce says, "Let's call it a day." (time to go home.)

Glossary

let's go pig out

Definition: to eat a lot

Language Usage:

"Let's go pig out" is an idiom
(An idiom is a phrase that means something different than the literal words being used. Examples: "It is raining cats and dogs" means it is raining very hard and "Go break a leg!" means go try your hardest.)

Evidence of how the word is used in the story.

Lexie says to Eduardo at lunchtime, "Let's go pig out (go eat a lot). I am starving!"

one tough cookie

Definition: a person who is confident, brave, and will stand up for themself

Language Usage:

"one tough cookie" is an idiom
(An idiom is a phrase that means something different than the literal words being used. Examples: "It is raining cats and dogs" means it is raining very hard and "Go break a leg!" means go try your hardest.)

Evidence of how the word is used in the story.

When Lexie tells Jason, the bully, to stop being mean he says, "Lexie, you are one tough cookie" (not someone to mess with.)

Glossary

raining cats and dogs

Definition: it's raining really hard

Language Usage:

"raining cats and dogs" is an idiom
(An idiom is a phrase that means something different than the literal words being used. Examples: "It is raining cats and dogs" means it is raining very hard and "Go break a leg!" means go try your hardest.)

Evidence of how the word is used in the story.

When Eduardo and Lexie are walking in the hallway to get lunch, they look out the window and hear kids talking about how it is raining cats and dogs (raining really hard.)

resilient

Definition: doesn't stop trying; keeps practicing to get better at something; recovers quickly; stamina

Part of Speech:

This word is a (noun, adjective, verb, adverb).

Evidence of how the word is used in the story.

When Eduardo is working on his English with Mrs. Bryce, he is resilient (keeps trying; not giving up.)

Glossary

skedaddle

Definition: to leave, run away in a hurry; flee

Part of Speech:

This word is a (noun, adjective, verb, adverb).

Evidence of how the word is used in the story.

At the end of the day, Mrs. Bryce tells the class to skedaddle (leave for the day.)

surrendering

Definition: to turn over or yield to the power or control of another; to give oneself up to someone or something; submit, forfeit

Part of Speech:

This word is a (noun, adjective, verb, adverb).

Evidence of how the word is used in the story.

Jason, the bully, surrenders (gives up his power and quits being mean) to Lexie when she sticks up for herself and Eduardo.

Glossary

taunts

Definition: to make fun of, tease, or challenge using mean language.

Part of Speech:

This word is a (noun, adjective, verb, adverb).

Evidence of how the word is used in the story.

Jason taunts (makes fun of, is mean to) Eduardo when he first meets him.

tricky

Definition: not easy: needing skill or care; difficult

Part of Speech:

This word is a (noun, adjective, verb, adverb).

Evidence of how the word is used in the story.

Mrs. Bryce tells Lexie that English can be tricky (not easy, difficult) to understand.

unsure

Definition: not confident; worried; not certain; having doubt

Part of Speech:

This word is a (noun, adjective, verb, adverb).

Evidence of how the word is used in the story.

Mrs. Carlton, the lunch lady, is unsure (not confident, worried) when she tries to speak Spanish to Eduardo in the lunch line.

About the Author: Kim Dawson

I am a single mom of two wonderful kids. I have been teaching for a number of decades and love spending time with my students. I have been writing since I was a child. It has always been a way for me to express myself when I am struggling. I strongly believe that we do not give our kids the credit they deserve. They have a lot to teach us if we just listen.

About the Illustrator: Paige Anocibar

Art is my passion. Every day I am thankful to have a career that empowers me to express myself through creativity. Drawing has been a part of my life since I was a small child. Coloring and painting were my favorite part of going to school. Back then, just like now, I was eager for the next art project. I knew that expressing myself through art is all I have ever wanted to do with my life, and illustrating this book has helped me achieve a part of that dream.

If you enjoyed this story, see other books in this Children's Leadership series, Living Love Forward.

2023 Books

| February | May | September | November |

2024 Books

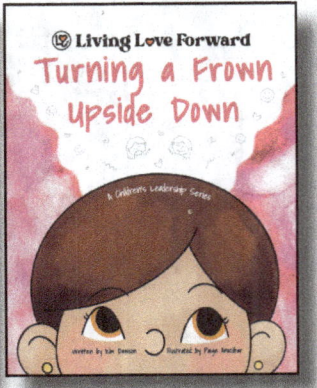

| March | May | September | November |